★ PAWTRIOT ★
DOGS

SAVE THE SANCTUARY

by Samuel P. Fortsch
illustrated by Manuel Gutierrez

GROSSET & DUNLAP

I dedicate this book to the brave men and women of the
US Armed Forces. And to my wife, Julia, and our kids
Samuel, William, and Madeline. And last but
not least: my parents—SPF

In memory of Copito, Colita, Toby, Nuky, Flavor, Hermes,
Orson, Jay Boy, and John Fitzgerald Tinta—MG

GROSSET & DUNLAP
An Imprint of Penguin Random House LLC, New York

Photo credit: cover: (paper background): darkbird77/iStock/Getty Images Plus

Text copyright © 2020 by Samuel P. Fortsch. Illustrations copyright © 2020 by Penguin Random House LLC. All rights reserved. Published by Grosset & Dunlap, an imprint of Penguin Random House LLC, New York. GROSSET & DUNLAP is a registered trademark of Penguin Random House LLC. Printed in the USA.

Visit us online at www.penguinrandomhouse.com.

Library of Congress Cataloging-in-Publication Data is available upon request.

ISBN 9780593222331   10 9 8 7 6 5 4 3 2 1

CHAPTER 1
AIRBORNE

Location: Classified
Date: 15AUG18
Time: 1800 hours

Welcome aboard, recruit!

Things move fast in the Army, so let me *debrief* you. That's Army-talk for "getting you up to speed on the details of the mission . . . and quickly."

We're about to jump out of a C-130 Hercules—

that's a big plane! A four-engine turboprop military transport aircraft to be exact.

We're cruising at an altitude of one thousand feet and zooming through the sky at 115 knots—that's more than 130 miles an hour—above the rain forest.

The thick trees and dense fog will make this jump even more dangerous, so we have to stay extra focused. We're linking up with US troops on the ground at *RP1*. That means Rally Point 1— our first checkpoint. The troops are en route to a small farming village deep inside the forest.

We've received intel reports that the enemy has forced the villagers out of their homes and taken the land for themselves. The enemy then placed hidden explosive traps around the village to keep us out. And that's why we're here: to find and safely disarm the explosive traps and return the land to the villagers. It's rightfully their land and it's our job to make sure it stays that way.

Now, I bet you're wondering: *Who is this crazy dog and why is he about to jump out of a perfectly good airplane???*

I'm Sergeant Ricochet. Rico for short. I'm a Belgian Malinois, and I'm a soldier in the United States Army. I was born for this life. Really . . . I was! Back at Lackland Air Force base in Texas two years ago. That makes me fourteen in human years.

And that's where I met her: Kris, my handler,

the woman I'm strapped to. She chose me out of twenty other pups at the base. She said it was because I had so much energy, like a pinball "ricocheting" around the room . . . and the name just stuck!

For the last two years, Kris taught me everything there is to know about sniffing bombs, bad guys, and bacon! She's trained me since the day I was born. Okay, I didn't *actually* get trained to sniff meats, but I *absolutely* love, love, love bacon. And Kris knows it, too. She always gives me hers because she's a vegetarian.

Kris also taught me the Soldier's Creed. It's the code that she and I live by. It's what all soldiers in the United States Army live by. It keeps us focused and determined so we can do our job and complete the mission—no matter the situation.

Between the roar of the C-130's big engine and the whipping of the wind outside, it's hard to even think, let alone stay calm. But that's part of the Soldier's Creed: *I am disciplined, physically and mentally tough, trained and proficient in my warrior tasks and drills.* It's our job to stay calm in the face of danger. And it's our duty to place the mission first.

Kris gives me a squeeze and a peck on the head, and I know it's time to jump. She checks and tightens my straps on the parachute. I slobber her with my tongue to let her know how much I love jumping out of airplanes.

"When we jump, count to four, then pull the ripcord on the parachute," Kris says while sliding the door open. The cold, wet air rushes into the plane.

"Hooah!" I howl. That's Army-talk for "let's go!"

And just like that, we're hurtling down toward earth at almost 120 miles per hour!

"One . . ."

"two . . ."

"three . . ."

"four!"

★ ★ ★

Time: 1815 hours

We hit the ground. Hard.

Kris secures our gear and detaches me. It's time to get to work!

We landed in a muddy pig farm on the outskirts of the village, fifty meters from RP1.

My first priority is to scan the area. That's a soldier's natural instinct when we're in an unknown location.

It is late evening and the sun is about to set over the trees, but it's just enough light to get a clear scan of my surroundings. I can see a faint light in the distance coming from some of the villagers' homes, which are thatch hutches made from trees.

I finish my initial scan. Not much to see here: no bad guys, no bombs, and aside from the pigs, there's definitely no bacon!

We link up with the other soldiers. Kris looks at her map and calls out to me, "Rico, go left. We're half a klick from the bad guy's hideout."

Klick is Army-talk for "kilometer."

This way. *Hooah!*

Time: 1845 hours

I've got the village in my sight. Let's move out.

I watch as Kris uses hand and arm signals to silently communicate with the rest of the soldiers. They follow her signal and we all start to stealthily crawl through the grass toward the village.

I have so many different smells coming into my nose: the dirt, the trees, the air, the sweat dripping

off the soldiers. I can still smell the pigs and they're half a klick away! I smell everything, but what I'm sniffing for is chemical powder, TNT, or dynamite. These smells alert me (and Kris) to where the enemy has hidden the explosive traps. Our intel reports show that they have set up ten bombs around the village.

I stop and close my eyes to focus all of my attention to my nose. I breathe in and out quickly, lowering my nose to the ground.

And then, just like that, I've got a scent. My ears perk up and I look to Kris. She knows I'm on to something. She begins following me—quietly and closely—as we march through thick, wet mud. I'm filthy, but it doesn't stop me: We've got a mission to do. We move quickly through the terrain, passing thickets and shrubs, following the scent.

Then I stop.

I motion with my head and point with my nose to an innocent-looking pile of leaves and twigs. But I know it's anything but innocent. I watch as Kris approaches the pile and slowly begins to remove the leaves . . . revealing a trip-wire bomb.

Kris carefully cuts the wire and we keep moving. She pats me on the head to let me know I did a good job. We would have been toast.

We continue making our sweep around the village, uncovering bomb after bomb. Kris silently motions out to the soldiers to "set up a perimeter." This means to arrange themselves in a big circle to keep us safe while we finish our sweep looking for bombs. In all, we uncover nine. Sometimes intel reports aren't 100 percent accurate.

We begin surrounding the enemy forces. They take one look at us and know they are outnumbered. We watch as they quickly retreat into the dark.

Finally, when we make it to the edge of the village, the villagers come out of hiding in the forest and greet us with smiles and hugs. They invite us to stay for dinner.

★ ★ ★

Time: 1930 hours

I watch as they build a fire and begin roasting one of the wild hogs. We sit around the fire and the villagers sing songs for us. What a great day to be in the Army. The villagers get to keep their land and we get to load our bellies up with some *hot chow*! That's Army-talk for "food."

While the villagers are singing and my fellow soldiers are relaxing, I catch another scent.

It's so potent, so overwhelming. It's absolutely intoxicating.

I begin following the trail. It smells like . . .

BACON!

But I can't slow down when there's . . .

By the time I realize it's not bacon, it's too late.

CHAPTER 2
A NEW LIFE

Location: Washington, DC, United States
Date: 25JUN20
Time: 0900 hours

It's been almost two years since the bomb went off. The explosion was so loud that for two weeks all I could hear was a ringing in my ears.

The last thing I remember was being pulled out of the rubble. Then it was four long weeks recovering in the hospital. The blast took away my front left leg and my sense of purpose. And worst of all, it took Kris away from me.

I don't think I'll ever get used to this place, this world, a world without Kris, a world without the Army. I'm not upset with the Army. I had served my time, and served it honorably, but I just couldn't put the uniform back on. I felt ashamed about the mission. They tried to help me, but I wouldn't listen. They had no choice but to discharge me.

And that's the truth: The Army's got no need for a three-legged pooch. They patted me on the head, sent me packing, and the next thing you know, I found myself living on the streets of Washington, DC, our nation's capital.

Still, every morning when I wake up from a dream, I open my eyes and can't believe I ended up *here,* all because I lost my military bearing and let my guard down . . . chasing what I thought was a piece of bacon. I don't even care for bacon anymore.

They call it the "Sanctuary," whatever that's supposed to mean. All I know is it's an animal shelter for rejects like me, without a mission. I used to be special. I used to have a job. But now? I'm just like everyone else here.

There's an English bulldog around here named Brick, who is just about the laziest dog you will ever meet. Story goes he overslept one morning and missed his flight back to England, where he's from. He's so lazy he decided to just stay here. He speaks with this funny Cockney accent. That's a British accent. He's always saying *"Oi!"* which sounds like *boy* without the *b*.

I'm not the only Army dog here, either. There's a rottweiler named Truman who served overseas with the Missouri National Guard. He lost his vision in a training accident four or five years back and doesn't talk much.

And then there's Penny: I'm not sure what's wrong with her, but she's *way* too happy and cheerful for a place like this. She's a black lab who was born here, so she doesn't know anything better than this place. Penny runs the Sanctuary with Ms. Becca, the lady who owns it.

Penny loves the Sanctuary—maybe a little *too* much. She thinks that everyone here is just "perfect." But I always say, "If we're so perfect, then why are we here?" She usually just laughs and says, "Rico, stop being so silly."

But I know she knows I'm not being silly. She knows I'm serious. And she knows why I'm always sad.

And no, it's not because I lost my leg. I'm sad because that day was the last day I ever saw Kris. That was the last day I ever felt happiness in my heart. And that was the last day I felt a sense of purpose. I still don't know what happened to Kris. I just hope she's okay. I think about her every day in this no-good, stinking place.

There's not much else to do here, except for sit around. Penny says if you look close enough you can see the White House. Beats me, though, I've never tried. What's the point?

I've been at the Sanctuary for a little over a year now. The only reason I know this is because Penny wanted to throw me a one-year anniversary party, but I told her I didn't want one.

I was just fine on my own, sleeping outside and eating scraps wherever I could find them. You'd be surprised at how much food people throw away and how good it still tastes. Most of it's better than the MREs we ate in the Army. MRE stands for "meal ready to eat."

Or as Kris used to say, "Meal, rarely edible." She always knew how to make me smile. I miss her laugh.

The streets of DC can be fun and I got to know them like the back of my paw. I actually liked living outside. We did it all the time in the Army. Then one day, I was minding my own business, trying to get some shut-eye in the alley behind this place when Penny and Ms. Becca came up to me.

"You're not sleeping outside, not one more night, you're coming with us to the Sanctuary," Penny said.

I told them to scram, leave me alone, but Penny wouldn't listen.

"Come on inside. We'll fix you up and get you a nice meal and a bed," Penny said.

Fix.

I really can't stand that word. It suggests I'm broken. Well, maybe my spirit was broken. Maybe it still is. But just 'cause something's broken don't mean it needs fixing, now does it?

I knew the two of them wouldn't leave me alone. So I figured: *What have I got to lose?*

So, that was that. And here we are. This is my life now. I'm surrounded by a bunch of dogs, cats, snakes, and birds that have only one thing in common: No one wants them.

There's even a skunk here. His name is Jean Claude, but everyone calls him Stripes, on account of that big white stripe across his back. Real original.

Brick is Penny's assistant. Penny, of course, thinks he's just "perfect." He's a perfect lazybones— that's what he is. For the last month, all Penny talks about is the Fourth of July parade coming up.

Every year she has everyone gather by the fence to watch the parade go by. She even makes a seating chart to make sure the little ones can see. Penny says she loves the different displays of patriotism. Or as she calls it, "*paw*-triotism." Again, real original.

I didn't watch last year, and I definitely won't watch this year.

★★★

Oh, great. Here they come now.

"Hiya, Rico! How's your *fantastic* morning going?" Penny asks me, bubbly as her usual self.

Behind her is a trail of young puppies who just arrived from the puppy mill. Penny protects them like they're her own children.

"I didn't know it was fantastic," I say.

Penny looks at me like I'm crazy. Brick is half asleep, holding a clipboard with a list on it.

"Oh, stop it! This is the best place in the world. What more could you want?"

I don't seriously entertain her question, so I let her continue.

"So, no biggie, but Brick and I are working on the seating chart for the Fourth of July parade and were wondering if you might want—"

"*Negative,*" I say. That's Army-talk for "*no.*"

"But—" Penny pleads with me.

"I just want to be left alone," I tell her.

Penny starts to give me the "tilt"—it's her signature move. She turns her head so much it looks like it's about to fall off. She "tilts" when she doesn't like your answer or suspects something is out of the ordinary.

"Oh, come on! The more the merrier."

"You can barely even see the parade through the alley," I tell her.

"Some of us actually *prefer* the narrow view. And besides, where's your *paw*-triotism? You're a soldier, Rico!"

I shake my head side to side and look down at my missing leg. "Not anymore."

I watch as Brick puts a big "X" next to my name.

"Well, everyone wants you to watch with us," Penny says.

"Nobody cares if I watch," I say.

"*Oi!* Penny, are we finished here?" asks Brick, his Cockney accent extra thick this morning.

Penny just sighs.

"I'm starving and I need a nap. And then I'll need a post-nap snack. I'm useless if I'm tired and hungry," Brick says.

"Fine. Just go," Penny says. This is the first time I've seen Penny even slightly less cheery than her usual self.

I watch as Brick moseys away and finds a shady spot to sleep in. I figure this is the end of our chat, but instead, Penny leans in close to me and whispers, "Listen, Rico. I know the view of the parade stinks, but it's the best we've got. Everyone watches . . . and I mean *everyone*."

"Well, not me."

Penny shakes her head, defeated, and starts walking away. Then she stops and turns back around to me.

"Oh, and by the way, *I care*. I care if you watch. If you're living here at the Sanctuary under my roof, you're family. You always talk about your old unit, right? Well, you're a part of this one now. And this unit sticks together. This unit doesn't leave anyone behind. I'm not *quitting* on you."

I stood there, shaky on my three legs, and all I could think about was Kris. She loved fireworks on the Fourth. And then I thought about the Soldier's Creed she taught me: *I will never quit.*

Maybe Penny had a point: *Am I quitting on myself?*

Then again, I wasn't a soldier anymore.

CHAPTER 3
DARK CLOUDS

Location: Washington, DC, United States
Date: 4JUL20
Time: 1630 hours

I look up at the sky and all I see is gray. It has been like this all afternoon. I know the sun is up there somewhere, but its light can't make it through the heavy cloud cover.

The parade is starting soon, and everyone here is complaining about the weather even though the first drop of rain hasn't hit yet. Not Penny, though—she's always happy and never complains.

"If it ain't raining, we ain't training." That's what we used to say in the Army. I bet Penny would have been a great Army dog. She's got plenty of spirit, that's for sure. And plenty of persistence. She's still trying to convince me to watch.

Penny says that on account of the parade, we have some extra visitors coming to the Sanctuary, and not the good kind. Matter of fact, it's the worst kind. It's Hans and Heinz, a pair of feisty Doberman pinschers. They're the two meanest dogs you'll ever meet. And they'll be with their owner, Mr. Mocoso, who's just about the cruelest human to exist. The three of them are perfect for one another. Most of the animals run for cover and hide when they show up. Last week, Hans and Heinz found Brick's hidden stash of treats and made him watch as they ate it all.

If Kris were here, she would say, "embrace the suck"—meaning "deal with it." But some days that's easier said than done.

Mr. Mocoso always wears a pressed white suit that matches his pale skin but he's all dark on the inside. He wears these big round red glasses. They're like shutters for the windows to his soul . . . if he had one. He's very tall, but even still, his pinschers look like giants. And he's got this big scar on his neck. Rumor has it that Mr. Mocoso's last pet, a monkey named Simon, turned on him and took a bite out of his neck. Penny says Mr. Mocoso started it. She said he grabbed Simon by the throat and squeezed him so hard that he turned blue. Simon managed to escape and nobody's heard or seen him since.

Mr. Mocoso's mom used to run the Sanctuary before Ms. Becca took over. Something must have happened between him and his mom, because he absolutely *loathes* this place and everyone inside of it. Some of the other animals think it's because nobody wants us as pets. I think they're giving him too much credit. He's just pure evil in my book. If he hates the Sanctuary so much, I wonder what he's doing here. I don't think he's here for the parade.

★★★

Time: 1700 hours

All of a sudden, the door swings wide open and out come Hans and Heinz, trotting over to me, noses high in the sky as they make their way into the yard. They always try to bully me. I stand up tall on my three legs to let them know I'm not scared.

"Would you look at this stupid thing, Heinz?" says Hans.

"Which thing? Everything here is stupid," Heinz replies.

"This *thing*, this three-legged freak," says Hans, pointing directly at me.

I usually just ignore them, but not today. The parade is about to start and it's about to rain. And I know if I don't stand up to them, they'll just target Penny next.

"Don't you two have some butts to sniff?" I say.

Hans and Heinz look at each other in shock. I'm a bit shocked at myself. That came out of nowhere. Maybe there is a little soldier left in me after all.

"Sounds even more stupid than he looks! Doesn't he, Heinz?"

"Very stupid, Hans."

They start approaching me, but I stand my ground. Hans presses his big wet snout against mine, but I don't back down. Then he pushes me. I stumble to the ground because I don't have the balance I used to without a front leg.

Of course they start howling with laughter. The laughter catches the ear of Penny, who now comes over to watch.

I stand back up straight and begin gritting my teeth. I can feel my blood boiling. And just as I'm about to snap at them . . . a piercing sound hits my ears.

"You heard your master's whistle. Time for you two to *move out*!" I say.

"Move out of what?" asks Hans.

"That's Army-talk for 'leave!'"

Heinz growls.

"Pipe down, tripod. I didn't hear a whistle. Did you, Hans?"

"Didn't hear a thing, Heinz."

"Well, maybe you two should consider getting your ears cleaned!" Penny chimes in.

I don't know if Penny was trying to be funny, but that made me double over with laughter. I could hear the other animals starting to join in. This was not something Hans and Heinz were used to, and the animals at the Sanctuary were enjoying every moment of it.

As the laughter was dying down, Hans started to crack a smile. At first I was surprised that he was embracing the joke—even if it was a silly one. But that wasn't the case. He was smiling for a different reason. A very bad one.

"You knuckleheads might be laughing now, but you won't be laughing when Mr. Mocoso shuts this place down," says Heinz.

The Sanctuary goes silent and no one is laughing anymore.

"That's right. It's over for all of you. Or as your friend tripod would say, 'It's time for you to MOVE OUT!'"

I look over to Penny. She is confused and starts doing the "tilt."

"Shutting down?" she says.

Hans has a big grin on his face and says, "Wait a second . . . you're telling me you don't even know . . . do you?"

"I thought you ran this place. What a joke!" Heinz chimes in.

"But Mr. Mocoso can't shut it down. The Sanctuary belongs to Ms. Becca," Penny says.

"That's what *you* think!" says Heinz.

"It can't be! Is Penny the brave actually showing signs of defeat? You look like you've seen a ghost! I can't say I blame you, Penny. You and your little family of rejects being taken from the only home you've ever known, it's quite sad," says Hans.

It's pouring rain now, so Mr. Mocoso blows his whistle again, even louder this time.

"All right, fellas," I say. "The whistle means *leave.* You don't want to wind up like Mr. Mocoso's last pet, now do you?"

This catches their attention and they slowly begin to leave, but not before Hans can shout, "Better start packing . . . and soon! The Snatchers are on their way now."

The Snatchers.

When they mention the Snatchers, the other animals look worried. I'm worried, too. The Snatchers are bad news. The Snatchers are big, burly men with beards to match their size.

And just as Hans and Heinz leave, the door opens and we're surrounded.

Penny stands in front of the door, protecting the younger puppies, but it's no use. The Snatchers are fast, efficient, and ruthless. And we've got no escape.

I've had close run-ins with them on the streets before, but I always had an escape plan. There are nine of them and they're blocking the only exit we have. They make quick work of us. I watch, helplessly, as they snatch up each of my fellow animals with pole nets and lock them up in cages, one by one. Penny, Brick, Truman, and even Stripes—every last one of them.

They've all got one-way tickets to the city pound—every animal's worst nightmare.

And I'm next.

CHAPTER 4
THE POUND

Location: Somewhere in Washington, DC
Date: 5JUL20
Time: 0800 hours

I can barely see in here. It's cold and dark and smells like they haven't cleaned in weeks. When I arrived, one of the Snatchers said, "Welcome to the pound!" but I think they brought us to the city dump. I used to love my powerful nose.

"Rico can sniff a bomb from a hundred klicks away," Kris used to brag to all of the soldiers. Now I wish I couldn't smell at all.

The worst part about being here—wherever *here* is—is that we missed the parade. Not that I really cared to see it, but I know how much it meant to Penny.

There are mostly dogs and a handful of cats here. They all look very tired and sad. Who wouldn't? We're all crammed into this tiny room in the cellar that feels like a prison.

The younger puppies haven't stopped crying since we got here yesterday. Penny tries to console them, but it's no use. Even they can tell there's no way out.

"Why would they take us from the Sanctuary? We didn't do anything wrong. Why can't we just go home, Penny?" I hear the puppies ask her.

Even Brick is complaining more than usual.

"I just want my bed back," he keeps saying.

I feel like I should say or do something to make them feel like there's hope, but then I'd be lying.

It is what it is. That's what we used to say in the Army. I try to let my mind wander and think about better times: when I was with Kris, when I was in the Army . . .

And suddenly, I hear a voice that jolts me from my thoughts.

"*Psst, psst,* hey, you."

I can hear but can't tell who said it. I stand up and turn around to try to figure out where it's coming from.

"*Psst, psst,* over here," I hear again.

I limp over to the corner of the cell past a clowder of cats and see an old bloodhound resting on the ground.

"Army, right?" he asks.

"How'd you know?" I say.

"Come on now. Plenty of signs. I saw you scanning the room, checking the situation the second you got here," he says.

I nod. I know when a dog's been in the military, too. And he's right; they trained us to "soak in our surroundings."

"That bulldog over there . . . ," he says.

"That's Brick. What about him?" I ask.

"He a friend of yours?"

"I suppose . . . ," I say with a bit of hesitation in my voice.

"Well, do you trust him?" the old hound asks.

"Who wants to know? How do I know I can trust you?" I ask him skeptically as I scan him up and down. He's heavy and out of shape. Definitely doesn't fit the build of an Army dog. He's missing a leg, too. But he has a prosthetic wheel where his leg used to be.

I can tell this guy is wasting my time, so I start to hobble away.

"Sergeant First Class Chaps wants to know. That's who."

I suddenly realize just who I'm talking to. I turn around and immediately straighten my posture and stance to show the old hound dog respect, since he outranks me. Sergeant First Class Chaps is a total legend. During his time in the Army, he sniffed out over 1,000 bombs and saved thousands of lives.

"My mistake, Sergeant. I didn't know who I was speaking with. I'm Rico."

But even though I didn't know who he was,

I should have treated him with dignity and RESPECT. It's one of the Army values that I'm supposed to live by.

"At ease, soldier," he says, so I relax my stance. "Got any rank attached to that name?"

"There was," I say.

"What do you mean, *was*? You Army or not?" he asks.

"I was a sergeant. Not anymore."

"Well, if you *was* then you *is*! Once a soldier, always a soldier."

I admire Chaps's tenacity, but I just don't feel like a soldier anymore. I still can't believe I'm standing in front of a legend like Chaps.

"What are *you* doing here?" I ask him.

"That's a story for another day. We don't have much time and I need your help."

Before I can get a word in, the cell door swings open and one of the Snatchers barges in. He blows right past Chaps and me and corners this old alley cat. We watch as the Snatcher grabs the helpless cat by the scruff of its neck and hauls it away. As quickly as the Snatcher came in, he is gone.

"What just happened?" I ask Chaps.

"Thirty days just happened. Poor cat's time was up."

And then I realize that this isn't just some ordinary city pound. No, this is a kill shelter. If an animal isn't adopted in thirty days, then that's the end of the line. No *ifs, ands,* or *buts.*

"Like I said, we're running out of time," Chaps says. "So, soldier, can you help me?"

CHAPTER 5
TIME IS TICKING

Location: Somewhere in Washington, DC
Date: 5JUL20
Time: 0850 hours

I know it's my duty to help another soldier who is in distress, but what can *I* do? We're trapped in this cold, dank dump and I can barely see, let alone find an escape route.

I know Chaps can sense my hesitation to help. "It's not just me who needs your help, soldier."

I watch as he looks up to the ceiling and lets out a soft whistle like a signal of sorts.

The pipes begin to shake and dust falls onto the floor. "Get down here, y'all," Chaps calls out.

Then, out of the shadows emerges something I've never seen in my life: a hedgehog riding a ferret and a rabbit riding a snake. They make their way to Chaps.

I do a double take because I cannot believe

my eyes. The hedgehog, ferret, rabbit, and snake all give Chaps a big, long group hug.

"This is my team. My unit. We call ourselves the Fellowship, and they've been trying to bust me out for thirty days," Chaps says.

Chaps motions to the hedgehog and says, "Show him."

The hedgehog unrolls a piece of paper and holds it in front of my face.

It reads "The Kill List" at the top and it's got today's date on it. Right below Chaps's name is Penny's. Mine is right below hers.

Seeing her name on that list really makes my heart hurt.

"I thought you said we had thirty days?" I ask Chaps.

"Y'all must have done *something* real bad or made *someone* real mad," said Chaps.

I can only think of one person who is evil

enough to have put Penny's name at the top of the list . . . *Mr. Mocoso*!

"We all need your help. Think you can do one last mission to help save your fellow animals?"

Before I can even consider Chaps's offer, Penny, Brick, and the other animals from the Sanctuary interrupt.

"Hiya, Rico. I hate to be a buttinsky, but we need to get out of here . . . and fast," Penny says.

"I know, Penny. But what do you want me to do? I thought Ms. Becca was coming to save us," I say.

"Rico, if you can just get us outside, you can lead us home. You know the streets so well!" Penny says.

And then a bunch of the other animals from the Sanctuary gather around.

"What are we going to do, Rico?" one asks.

"Rico, we have to do something! The Sanctuary is our home. We can't just let Mr. Mocoso take it," Penny says.

"Why does everyone think *I* know what to do?"

Even Stripes, the skunk who I've barely spoken

to in the last year, says, "Because you're the most courageous dog we know, Rico."

"What do you know about me?" I ask Stripes.

He's silent.

"What makes you think *I'm* courageous?" I ask him again.

"Because you were a sergeant in the Army. You have to be courageous in the Army, right?"

Now I'm the one who's silent. He is right, but I don't know what to tell him.

Chaps chimes in to break my silence: "He's right. I know you got some fight left in you. So listen up, ya'll, 'cause I'm the pooch with the plan."

"What's your plan?" Penny asks Chaps.

"For starters, I've got a way out. And your bulldog friend is just what we need," Chaps says.

"Brick?" Penny asks.

"Yes, ma'am, he's the perfect size," Chaps says.

"We need more than just a way out," says Penny.

"You name it," Chaps says.

"We need you to help us save the Sanctuary."

The hedgehog interjects: "This isn't part of the plan, Chaps!"

"Well, neither was me being chased by those dogs and getting stuck in here for thirty days. And since I'm on tonight's list, we need the bulldog's help . . . and Rico here knows the streets."

"The dog with three legs is going to lead us?" asks the hedgehog.

"Hey! Enough with that. I'm missing a leg, too, but you don't question me, now do you?"

"Yeah, but you have a wheel—"

"I said enough," Chaps says. "Have I ever let you down?"

"You're right, Chaps, sorry. We'd follow you to the ends of the Earth."

"They'll need someone with your training and leadership skills. Someone who knows the streets. They'll be dead meat on their own," Chaps says to me.

"Then let's hurry! The Snatchers will be back any moment!" says the hedgehog.

I know they're all counting on me, but I don't feel like leader I used to be.

CHAPTER 6
A NEW HOPE

Location: Somewhere in Washington, DC
Date: 5JUL20
Time: 0945 hours

"You see that busted up vent in the bottom of the wall over there?" Chaps says to me.

"The one with the bolts?" I ask.

"Yes, but don't worry about those bolts. That's what they're for," Chaps says, pointing to the hedgehog and rabbit.

I watch as the hedgehog and rabbit begin unscrewing the bolts on the vent.

Chaps continues, "More importantly, we need Brick to ram through that vent. Even without the bolts, it's practically sealed shut. And once it opens, you mustn't stop running. I repeat, we *cannot* get through that vent without Brick." Chaps and I watch as they continue to work on the vent. Then, Chaps asks them, "How's it coming?"

"I need another minute or two . . . ," says the hedgehog.

Then, out of the corner of my eye, I see the door beginning to open.

"Guys, we've got company. We may not have another minute," I say to the group.

The Snatcher is walking down the hallway, heading straight for our cell. I watch as he takes out his keys, turns the knob, and pushes the gate. It starts to swing open, when all of a sudden Penny charges forward. She slams the gate shut and knocks the Snatcher to the ground.

But the Snatcher pops right back up onto his feet and pushes back hard on the gate as Penny digs her paws in.

"I can't hold it any longer!" Penny yelps.

"You must!" the hedgehog cries out as she fumbles with the bolts.

We're running out of time. I realize that I have to do something and I have to act now. I can't let Penny down. I need to keep her safe.

"Follow me!" I say.

I move as fast as I can, practically falling into

the gate next to Penny. The rest of the pets rush in and help barricade it shut. More Snatchers arrive and push with all their weight, slowly moving us back inch by inch.

"How are we looking?" I call out to the group.

"Almost there, just a little longer!" says the hedgehog.

"Hold your ground. Dig in!" Chaps calls out to me like he's giving me military orders.

I dig deep inside and hold my ground. I watch as the hedgehog rips the last bolt out.

"All right, where's that battering ram?" Chaps yells out.

Penny pokes her head through the pile of pets. "Brick!" she calls out.

I look over to Brick and he's dead asleep.

"WAKE UP!" I howl.

Nothing.

Penny pulls his eyelids back. "*Oi!* Wake up!"

"Can't you see I'm napping?" says Brick.

"We need you to knock down that vent!"

"Maybe later," Brick says and shuts his eyes again, returning to sleep.

I can feel the door shaking.

"There is no later, Brick! Knock it down now or I'll cut off your treats supply!"

In a flash, Brick pops to his feet, builds up a head of steam, and barrels through the vent. I've never seen him move that fast before.

"We're in business, everyone. Move! Move! Move!" Chaps calls out to us like troops.

I feel a new sense of urgency and purpose as we army crawl our way through the vent and begin making our escape to the outside world.

CHAPTER 7
TACTICAL WITHDRAWAL

Location: Outside of Pound
Date: 5JUL20
Time: 1000 hours

We're in the back of the pound in the lot where the Snatchers park their trucks. There is a long chain-link fence that serves as a major obstacle for our escape. On top of the fence is barbed wire so we can't just climb over. I watch as the hedgehog and the rabbit instinctively begin gnawing through the chain-link fence while the snake and ferret pull it apart to make a hole.

"Over here. Help me move this. We can use it as a barricade to secure the door," Chaps says to me, motioning to a dumpster with wheels.

I push all my weight against it, but it's hard with a missing front leg. Still, we've almost managed to position the dumpster to block the hole they just created in the chain-link fence so the Snatchers can't reach us, when all of a sudden . . .

The Snatchers budge the dumpster, but they're too big to fit through the hole. They keep pushing and pushing, but Chaps and I dig in even harder to make sure we keep the other animals safe from their long poles.

"You're up!" Chaps says to Penny.

"No, I'll go last," she says.

I'm behind Chaps as he makes his way through the hole with ease. I'm up.

I begin making my way through the hole in the fence. I can feel the exposed chain-link fence scratch the sides of my belly, but I keep pushing. My back paw gets snagged on the fence and I topple over, but Penny pushes me from behind, helping me make it through.

Now Penny is up. I turn around to make sure she gets through safely but behind her all I see is a big, long pole with a net at the end.

"*Oi!* Grab her, Rico!" Brick calls out to me.

I reach my front paw out through the hole, but I can't get a good grip on her with just one paw.

"Help me, Rico!" she howls.

"I'm trying! Just hold on," I say.

But I can feel my grip slipping. My heart is beating fast and all I can think about is Kris and the explosion.

I watch as my paw slips away from Penny's.

Out of nowhere, Chaps sticks his wheel out and Penny bites down on it.

"Pull us, y'all!" he calls out.

Brick and the others drag us out of there and we flee down the back alley.

"Follow me," I say. "I know a secret hiding spot in the basement of this old abandoned warehouse."

I lead everyone through the dark alley filled with overflowing trash cans, old tires, and broken wooden pallets. But all I can think about is how I almost got Penny caught and how they would be better off without me. I worry that all I'm doing is slowing them down.

★★★

Location: Abandoned Warehouse
Date: 5JUL20
Time: 1030 hours

There are cobwebs everywhere and rusty nails sticking out of the floorboards. There's a hole in the ceiling letting a small sliver of light from the moon into the room. Chaps uses this beam of light as a makeshift rally point as we catch our breath.

"Let me introduce y'all to my friends," says Chaps.

The hedgehog steps into the light and does a curtsy.

"My name is Franny and this fabulous ferret here is my best friend and loyal steed, Sawyer."

"Pleasure," says Sawyer as he joins Franny and Chaps.

"And my snake friend over here is—"

The snake enters the light with the bunny on his back.

"I'll introduce myssself, thank you very much. I'm Sssmithersss," he says as he bows his head. "And the fuzz ball on top of me can ssspeak for herssself."

The bunny waves. "My name's Morgan and it is very nice to meet you all."

Franny, the hedgehog, puts her arm around

Chaps and says, "So, my dear old friend, do you care to share any bits of this mission you've volunteered us for?"

"I don't know the details. That's where Rico comes in. So, Sergeant Rico, what's the plan?"

All eyes are on me. Penny, Brick, Franny, Morgan, Smithers, and Sawyer. They all want a plan, but I've got nothing.

So I pull Chaps aside and whisper in his ear, "Listen, Chaps. I respect you and everything you've done and everything you're trying to do for these animals, but I'm not who you think I am. I'm not a soldier anymore. And I definitely don't have what it takes to lead a mission. I'm so slow I almost just got us caught. I'll just stay behind with Truman and Stripes and protect the puppies."

Chaps takes a long, deep breath. "Rico, do you remember the values they taught us at boot camp? Loyalty, duty—" he says.

"Chaps, I didn't forget the seven Army values," I cut him off. "L.D.R.S.H.I.P.: Loyalty. Duty. Respect. Selfless Service. Honor. Integrity. Personal Courage."

"Well, those values don't just go away because you stop wearing the uniform or because you lost a leg. They're forever a part of your character. Look at me: I'm missing a leg, too. I've been exactly where you are. I know you want to give up on yourself. You want to lie around and do nothing. I get it. It's easy to do nothing. But you're a soldier. And once a soldier, always a soldier. I promise you, it gets better. But soldiers don't give up on themselves and they don't give up on their fellow animals. I know right now it's tough, but I need you to embrace the suck. You're a warrior, Rico. You always have been and always will be. Now, can I count on you?"

I stood up proud and tall on my three legs and looked around the room at all the animals' faces.

All I could say was *"Hooah!"*

CHAPTER 8
ZOOLOGICAL

Location: Abandoned Warehouse
Date: 5JUL20
Time: 2000 hours

We used the last several hours to rest up before the mission. I gather everyone around in a huddle just like we used to do in the Army. I was beginning to feel a new sense of purpose. A rush of adrenaline ran through me just like it used to before I would jump out of a plane.

"First, we need to get into Mr. Mocoso's mansion," I begin.

"Who is Mr. Mocoso?" Franny asks.

"He's the jerk who wants to close down the Sanctuary," Penny says.

"And what'sss that?" asks Smithers.

"It's our home and it means the world to Penny," I say.

"And we're to sssave it how?" asks Smithers.

"By telling the truth," Penny says.

I look around the room and can see everyone is confused.

Penny continues: "Mr. Mocoso is lying. He doesn't actually own the shelter."

This catches their attention, and Franny perks up. "Who is the rightful owner?"

"Ms. Becca is," Penny says. "Well . . . technically it's this guy named Will. But it sounds like he's best friends with Becca and he practically gave her the Sanctuary. And Mr. Mocoso was clearly upset with this arrangement so that's why he is claiming he's the rightful heir. I think he's sending all of us to the pound so he can close it and sell it for money."

I watch as Chaps leans back. I can tell he is skeptical of all this.

"Where is all this *intel* coming from?"

"Intel?" Penny asks.

"It's Army-talk. In other words, 'how do you know all of this'?" Chaps says.

"A few weeks back, this guy I had never seen before came in to the Sanctuary. He was wearing a really nice suit. It was right after Mr. Mocoso's mother died. The guy in the suit kept talking about 'Will' and how he holds the details about who owns the Sanctuary," Penny tells Chaps.

"Let me get this straight," Chaps says. I can tell he doesn't like the sound of all this. "So some guy came in, who you don't know, but he was wearing a suit and said that Will knows who is in charge."

"That's correct," Penny says.

"This doesn't sound like solid intel. What do you think, Rico?"

"I trust Penny," I say.

"That's good enough for me," Chaps says. "So where is this Will guy?"

"Well, I'm not sure, exactly, but I know who might know his whereabouts. Does anyone know how to get to the zoo?" Penny asks.

"I do," I say. "I used to get medicine from there all the time. We can take a shortcut through the sewers."

"Negative," says Chaps.

"What's wrong with the sewers?" I say.

"Besides sludge and garbage, rats, bats . . . ," says Penny.

"Can we *please* take the long way?" Brick asks.

"I'm not afraid of rats or bats. It's the Beast I'm afraid of," says Chaps.

"That's a fairy tale," Franny says.

"Sure isn't. I've seen the Beast with my own two eyes and even had a few close calls with him. And there's no way we are going through the sewers," Chaps says. "No way, no how. We'd never make it out alive."

Location: The Zoo
Date: 5JUL20
Time: 2045 hours

I can smell the zoo from here. We're less than a klick away. Our objective is simple: locate Mr. Mocoso's exiled pet Simon and pump him for intel on Will's location. Penny says he'll help because he doesn't like Mr. Mocoso. She reminds me that he's the monkey who took a bite out of Mr. Mocoso's neck.

I motion to the group to signal "follow me" and lead them to my secret entrance to the zoo.

We huddle up against the fence using the trees and bushes for cover.

"I'm taking Penny with me. Chaps, you hold down the rear here," I tell them.

Chaps gives me a *north south*. That's Army-talk for "nodding your head when you understand something."

"I could use the rest," he says.

"The primates are close. We'll be back in five mikes," I say. *Mikes* is Army-talk for "minutes."

Penny helps me wriggle through a hole in the fence and we move as fast as we can to the monkey and marmoset enclosure.

It's dark, but the moon casts a nice glow, and I can see the marmosets sleeping. Marmosets are funny-looking monkeys. They have silky hair with manes on either side of their faces. They aren't much bigger than Franny.

Penny starts quietly calling out "Simon?" but no one responds.

I watch as she trips over one, waking him up. "You're not Simon. Go back to bed. This is just a dream," whispers Penny.

All of a sudden, I hear rustling coming from the canopy of trees and see a monkey moving.

He climbs down the tree, effortlessly swinging from limb to limb.

In a flash, the little fella is on the ground and face to face with Penny.

"Simon! Oh, it is so good to see you," says Penny.

Simon quickly brings Penny in for a hug.

"I've missed you so much. How have you been, Simon?" asks Penny.

But Simon doesn't respond. He opens his mouth and speaks but in silence. Simon points to his throat and shrugs his shoulders.

"Your voice is gone?" asks Penny.

Simon nods "yes" and then points to me and tilts his head.

"This is Rico. He's helping us save the

Sanctuary. Mr. Mocoso shut it down," Penny says, and I watch as Simon's eyes fill with fear.

"That's why we're here," I tell him. "We're on a mission and we need intel on a guy named Will. Do you know his location?"

Simon's eyes relax and then he just laughs. He starts to use hand and arm signals to try and communicate with us.

"I don't know what you're saying," says Penny.

"I do," I tell Penny. I learned these hand and arm signals in the Army. Simon and I continue to communicate in silence and I start to get the answers we need.

I give Simon a thumbs-up to thank him for all the intel. Penny gives him a big hug and says goodbye.

But as we're leaving, I realize Simon could be a tactical asset on this mission.

"Come with us," I say.

Simon shakes his head "no."

"But you know the layout. You've done the recon," I say.

Simon points to some baby monkeys sleeping

up in the canopy. "I can't leave my babies," he signals to me.

"Understood. If you change your mind, you know where to find us," I say as we leave the zoo and make our way to the National Mall to link up with the rest of the group.

CHAPTER 9
BEWARE! THE SNATCHERS

Location: National Mall
Date: 6JUL20
Time: 2230 hours

The moon is full and bright, but the clouds are working hard to make it gloomy. When we were on nighttime missions in the Army, the soldiers would wear NVGs—night vision goggles. Not me, though. My eyes work just great in the dark. They're such a tactical asset.

I debriefed everyone on the will. Penny still can't believe a piece of paper determines who owns the Sanctuary. I could tell Chaps and obviously Brick were getting tired, so I offered up a shortcut, but Chaps insisted we stay aboveground. He swears the Beast is down there.

The good thing about taking the long way is that it's really nice around here. The National Mall has lots of memorials and statues. There's even a huge pool, and I can see our reflections as we walk by. I take a moment to look at our group. Though we're on a mission to find the will and stop Mr. Mocoso from closing the Sanctuary, we've got no uniforms, no formations, no military bearing, and no unit name. Every unit needs a name. It's a rallying cry!

I look over at Brick. He's huffing and puffing and clearly out of breath.

"Okay, I take it back. Can we *please* take the short way?" he asks.

"Would you stop whining?" says Franny.

"Don't get all spiky with me, you little porcupine," Brick quips back.

Franny laughs. "I actually belong to the order Erinaceomorpha."

"English, please," says Brick.

"I assure you, that was English. I'm a hedgehog, not a porcupine."

Brick rolls his eyes. "Same difference."

Penny chimes in, "Would you two cut it out? We need to keep our wits about us and stick together. And since we're a unit now, I want to let

you all know I've got a name for us."

Smithers snaps his head around. "Sssorry, but I ssspeak for the five of usss when I sssay our ssservices are only temporary. And asss sssuch, a name won't be necessary."

Penny shrugs and says, "Well, for the time being, and from now until forever, we shall henceforth, all of us, be known as—"

"*Oi!* Out with it," says Brick.

"The Pawtriots!"

Chaps turns to me and we smile at each other.

"That's a top tier name, Penny," Chaps says.

He's right. It's a great name.

We continue marching, making our way toward the Washington Monument. I can see the White House off in the distance, too. I begin thinking about whether I could actually see it from the Sanctuary. Maybe I'll give it a shot when I get back . . . if we save it.

Then, in the distance, I can see something, or someone, moving. I quietly whistle to Franny and she stops. Penny turns to me and whispers, "What is it?"

I scan the tree line about one hundred yards away and see shadows moving. I know exactly what *it* is.

"AMBUSH!" I howl. And as I say this, I see the Snatchers tear through the woods and start racing toward us. Three of them have hand cannons that shoot nets. A Snatcher fires one at us and I watch it fly through the air. It nearly hits Franny and Sawyer, but they manage to dodge it.

I look around for a place to hide, but we're completely exposed. The Snatchers are closing in on us, and I know I've got to take charge and make a tactical decision.

"Smithers, Morgan, *on me*!" I call out. That's Army-talk for "get over here!"

The two snap up and zoom over to me.

"Brick, Penny, I need mud balls, *now*!"

Brick is confused, and Penny gives me the "tilt," so I point to the ground and say, "Slobber and dirt!"

"Got it!" Penny says as she pulls Brick's tongue and lets his drool pour into the dirt.

"Sawyer, can you hold my weight?" I ask him.

"I assure you I am stronger than I look," Sawyer says back to me.

"Great. Okay, Morgan and Franny, I need you here and here," I say, directing them to assume positions about three feet apart.

"Hurry! They're closing in!" Franny says.

I see that the Snatchers sprinting toward us are only about fifty yards away now.

"Chaps, wheel to the sky!" I watch as Chaps doesn't even hesitate and gets right on his back with his wheel in the air.

"King of battle?" asks Chaps.

"Bingo," I reply.

King of battle is a nickname for the Army Artillery. And like we used to say in the Army, "Let's make it rain."

I take a moment to check the situation, and for the first time in a good, long while I feel like my old self again. The Rico that used to be in control. The Rico that used to be a leader. The Rico that was proud to be an Army dog.

The Snatchers are in striking distance, and I watch as Smithers wraps his head around Franny and his tail around Morgan. Then, Chaps pulls Smithers over his wheel like a slingshot and shouts, "Load!"

Penny puts a mud ball on top of Chaps's wheel and I yell out, "FIRE!"

We all watch as the mud ball hurls through the air and nails one of the Snatchers.

Direct hit!

"Reload!" I call out, and Penny quickly sends another one across the field, hitting another Snatcher in the face and sending him tumbling to the ground!

"Fire at will. I'm going to flank them with Sawyer!" I say to Penny. *Flank* is Army-talk for "charging at the enemy from the side."

The mud balls keep flying as Sawyer and I charge at the Snatchers from the left flank.

"Zig and zag, Sawyer," I say.

We weave in and out across the field as the Snatchers try to snag us with their nets. We're serving as a good distraction to keep the others safe—and we even manage to knock down a few of them—but there are just too many of them and they are closing in on us. We need an escape route. So I follow Sawyer back to the group.

"We have to fall back," says Chaps.

"But there's nowhere to go," Brick says.

"Then we take our chances with the rats," I say to them.

Chaps shakes his head and says, "I don't like this one bit, Sergeant."

I pause for a second and think about the Beast. I'm hoping Franny was right and that it's just a fairy tale.

"You put me in charge, remember?" I say.

Chaps cracks a smile.

I watch as Penny and Brick pop open a sewer grate. We all begin piling in. It's not the best option, but it is the only option. I'm the last to file in, and I hear the Snatchers' shouts begin to fade as we make our way lower into the sewers. All I can think of is rats and bats and, of course, the Beast. But I'm too old to believe in fairy tales, right?

CHAPTER 10
THE FOULS

Location: Underground
Date: 6JUL20
Time: 2300 hours

We make our way down the ladders and into the sludgy, murky water. I'm about paw-deep in the water, but I look back at Sawyer and Smithers and they are each up to their chin in sewage.

Gross!

I thought the smell in the pound was bad, but this is far worse. And it's even darker down here. I can barely see a foot in front of my face. But we're on a mission and I can't let that stop us. We've got to keep moving and get to Mr. Mocoso's mansion so we can find the will.

I look back to check on Chaps and can see he is walking slower than usual.

"Are you doing okay?" I ask him.

"I'm doing just fine," he says, but I know he's

not. This has been a long mission and it's definitely wearing on him.

"You don't have to lie to me, Chaps. I can see you're hurting."

He brushes me off and says, "I'm just an old dog with old dog problems. Focus on the rest of the Pawtriots, Sergeant."

"*Roger that,*" I tell him. That's Army-talk for "I get it."

"Oh, and Rico," Chaps says as he looks me dead in the eyes, "if we see that Beast, you better get this unit moving on the double."

I nod.

"I mean it. Y'all better haul some serious you know what."

"*I'm tracking,* Chaps." That's more Army-talk for "I'm following."

I speed up my pace a bit and call out to the others, "Pawtriots, let's keep it tight and let's keep it moving."

★★★

We're making some good progress and have yet to come across any rats or bats. Then Penny stops and calls me over. She found something.

"What is it?" I ask her.

"Looks like a switch of sorts."

I lean in close to get a better look. I can feel all the other Pawtriots right behind me trying to get a look, too. I blow some dust off the top of the switch and begin wiping it down, revealing the word ON.

Penny puts her paw on the switch and says, "Should I?"

"Maybe it's upside down and actually reads 'NO,'" Brick says.

"There's only one way to find out," I say.

I bring my paw to the switch and say, "On my count . . ."

"One . . ."

        "two . . ."

                "three!"

Suddenly, there is light and a legion of rats lining the walls! I see hundreds. Their fur bristles and their beady red eyes lock onto us.

"Pawtriots, RUN!" I say.

We begin barreling down the tunnels, sloshing through the sludge as the rats surround us on all sides.

"Which way?" Franny shouts out.

"Tunnel on the left!" Chaps directs.

We race through the tunnel as the rodent horde scurries down the pipes behind us. Penny looks on with horror at the disgusting infestation that's closing in.

"Brick, go faster!" Penny says.

"*Oi!* This is top speed!" he says.

We keep pushing our way through the tunnel and suddenly a deafening roar breaks the chaos of the chase.

I stop running and watch as the rats above me freeze in their tracks, too.

The ground shakes and the water ripples as a massive reptile, the size of a crocodile, covered in scars and sludge stomps his way toward us.

"It's the Beast! There's a ladder up ahead," Chaps yells out. "That fairy tale is our worst nightmare! Run!"

"Come on, Pawtriots! Double time!" I howl.

Franny leads the way and we begin booking it to what looks like an opening at the end of the tunnel. I'm hobbling as fast as I can, but then suddenly Franny shouts out, "STOP!" and we all pile up behind her, almost knocking her down.

"This is a dead end," she says, pointing out below her. I look down to where she is pointing and see a great big waterfall of sludge leading down to a pool of murky water almost fifty feet below.

"We're trapped," she says.

Chaps brings up the rear and looks down. "I'm sorry, y'all. I don't remember this," he says, his voice shaky. This is the first time I've seen him look concerned. He turns to me and says, "Just get

them to that ladder." I look across to the ladder—
it's at least a ten-foot jump to the other side and
below us is a fifty-foot drop.

"But—" I begin to say.

"No *buts*. You have your orders, Sergeant,"
Chaps says. Then I watch as he turns back around
and heads right toward the Beast.

"Where are you going?" I shout.

"I've got a bone to pick with him!" says Chaps
as he barrels toward the Beast.

★ ★ ★

Time: 2345 hours

I turn back to the group.

"I'll go first," Franny says without hesitation.
She sprints, leaps, and crash-lands on the other side
safely. I watch as Sawyer, Smithers, and Morgan do
the same—all without hesitation. Then Penny and
Brick jump to safety.

It's just me and Chaps. But Chaps is nowhere
to be found. I look down at my missing leg and
know this isn't going to end well.

"I'm going to go find Chaps!" I tell Penny.

But before I can take off, Penny shouts out, "Rico!" and points behind me. I turn around and see Chaps: he's exhausted, struggling to catch his breath, and has cuts all over his snout.

"Are you ready?" I ask him.

"Negative. I'm gonna see this one through," he says.

"What do you mean? We have to go, NOW!"

"I told you, I'm staying. I've got a bone to pick with this ugly reptile," Chaps says.

"Then I'll help you face him," I say.

Chaps gives me a big grin and shakes his head. "You can barely walk, let alone get enough speed to make that jump." Then he unbuckles his wheel leg and removes it.

"What are you doing?" I ask. "You won't make that jump without it."

"Neither will you," he says.

"Chaps, it doesn't have to end like this."

"Take the wheel, Rico. I'm passing it on to you so you can get across. It's time for you to lead them."

"You can't leave us—"

"No time for arguing. Just get the mission done," Chaps says as he puts the wheel leg on me.

"Find the will and save the Sanctuary. Now go!"

I take a few steps back to build up speed and begin running. The wheel is loose, but I feel alive again. The terrain is bumpy, but I don't let it faze me. I just keep running and running. I think about Kris and all the times we ran in and out of danger together. And I think about the Sanctuary and everyone who is counting on me as I'm about to jump and I hear a loud CRASH.

I land on the other side, my wheel still intact. I look behind me to see the Beast, that huge crocodile, smashing through the wall. The pipes burst, water rushes in, and debris flies everywhere. The pool of sludge rises below us, and across the way is Chaps.

He gives me a soldier's salute and turns to face the Beast. We all watch as he charges right at the massive reptile and lets out the loudest howl I've ever heard: "PAWTRIOTS!"

I knew that was the last time any of us would ever see Chaps. But he went out like a true soldier and put the mission first.

CHAPTER 11
KEEP MOVING

Location: Forest
Date: 6JUL20
Time: 0200 hours

We make our way up the ladder and out of the sewers onto a grassy hillside just outside the city where Brick, Morgan, and Smithers collapse to the ground, exhausted and crying. Penny goes over to give them each a big hug.

I want to go in for a hug, but there's no time: We're on a mission. *I will never quit.*

"Pawtriots, on your feet," I say to the group.

"Rico, please, give them a second!" Penny says back.

"We've got to get out of the open and into the woods before the sun comes up. Simon said Mr. Mocoso's mansion is just on the other side of the forest," I say.

"Rico's right," says Franny as she hops off of

Sawyer and wipes tears from her eyes. "Chaps was our friend, but he was also a soldier. He placed the mission first, without question." Franny walks over to me to give me a hug and says, "Now, let's straighten out this wheel. Penny, give me a paw, would you?"

"No, I can't wear this," I say, lowering my head to the ground as I start to take it off.

"Look at me, Rico," Franny says as she puts her paws on my cheeks and lifts my head back up.

I can hear Brick sniffling away his tears. "*Oi!* We can't have you wasting such a nice gift from Chaps."

Smithers slithers over to me and says, "We'll need you at top ssspeed, Sssergeant."

Penny shimmies the wheel back onto my leg as Franny tightens down the straps.

"Fits perfect," Penny says. "Let's move out, Pawtriots."

We clear off the hillside and make it through the woods at a good pace now that I have the wheel. It feels nice to have the wind in my face and steady ground beneath my feet again.

CHAPTER 12
MR. MOCOSO'S MANSION

Location: Outskirts of Mr. Mocoso's Mansion
Date: 6JUL20
Time: 0230 hours

It's going to be difficult to pull off a nighttime raid of Mr. Mocoso's mansion. Even if we breach the wall and get inside, we still have to get past those nasty pinschers, Hans and Heinz. The way I see it, we only have one shot to find the will and save the Sanctuary. There are lots of pets counting on us, and counting on me. I don't want to let them down.

I can see Mr. Mocoso's massive mansion all the way from here. It's a gray stone building covered in ivy and surrounded by a wrought iron gate. In the middle of the front lawn is a marble fountain with a statue of Mr. Mocoso with Hans and Heinz.

I scan the horizon and call everyone together. "Pawtriots, bring it in," I say.

"Yes, Sergeant. The Pawtriots are present and accounted for," Penny says as she gives me a nod.

"Let's go over the mission one last time," I say.

"Alpha team: Franny, Sawyer, Smithers, and Morgan. Bravo team: Penny, Brick, and myself."

"Tracking," the Pawtriots say to me in unison.

I continue, "Alpha team will provide us with an entry point through the perimeter. Once we get onto the lawn, remember to slow down and watch for booby traps. Rally Point 1 will be at the fountain. If security is on high alert like I expect it to be, we'll have to enter through the roof. Simon said that would be the best way in. Once inside the mansion, Bravo team will lead the search party, find the safe, extract the will, and exfil back to the fountain." (*Exfil* is Army-talk for "getting safely out of a dangerous area.") "Everybody tracking?"

They all nod.

"Good. And before we go, I just wanted to let you all know . . . ," I begin to say, but I can't seem to finish my sentence. I take a long, deep breath.

Brick huffs, "*Oi!* Out with it!" and everyone chuckles.

"Well, I wanted to say that when I lost my leg, I knew I would never be the same. I was sad because I didn't feel like me. Every time I looked down at where my leg used to be, it was a constant reminder of my failure to keep Kris safe. But you know what? If it hadn't happened, I would have never ended up at the Sanctuary and I would have never met all of you."

I watch as Penny begins to cry.

"I don't believe that's the conclusion of his speech," says Franny.

"It's not supposed to be a speech," I say.

"Sssurely sssounds like one to me," Smithers says.

"Sorry, I guess all I'm trying to say is thank you, and that I'm proud to be a Pawtriot."

"*Oi!* Now you're gonna make me tear up," Brick says.

"Better wipe those tears away, because it's GO time!" I say.

"Group hug first," says Penny.

We all bring it in for a hug and then begin making our way out of the forest.

Time: 0245 hours

We're sneaking across the lawn, moving very slowly. The entire lawn is full of booby traps. I can smell it. The rest of the Pawtriots are behind me, following my lead. We army crawl through the thick foliage, using shrubs as cover to get a better view of the terrain and stop when we reach the fountain.

I silently motion our unit to stop. I scan the situation. I see thick ivy climbing up the wall of Mr. Mocoso's mansion. And I can see Hans and Heinz inside, guarding a room.

I whisper, "We're gonna scale the ivy walls and enter through the roof."

"Are you sure?" Penny whispers back.

"It's our only option. There's a vent on the roof and we can use that to get in," I say as we begin to make our way to the side of Mr. Mocoso's mansion.

Time: 0300 hours

The vent is smaller than I hoped it would be, so we begin filing in one by one. Franny takes the lead and we all follow, shimmying our way through until we reach a ventilation shaft in the air duct.

She stops, turns around, and presses her finger to her lips, signaling for us to be quiet. Then she points below through the spinning blades of the ventilation fan.

I press my ear to the vent to listen to what they're saying. "Do you smell something?" I can hear Heinz ask Hans.

I watch as Hans brings his big snout high into the air up toward us and begins sniffing.

"Something smells rotten," Hans says.

"Keep an eye out," Heinz says back.

We carefully and quietly proceed until we reach the end of the passageway. Through the spinning blades I can see the two pinschers. The duct dumps us out on the ground floor, into Mr. Mocoso's bedroom. I take a scan of my surroundings: There are paintings of Mr. Mocoso with Hans and Heinz everywhere, but the house still somehow feels empty.

We look around, getting our bearings and hugging the dusty walls so we don't get spotted or sniffed out. This place is huge and we don't have much time.

I call the group in. "We need to split up," I whisper.

"Are you sure that's a good idea? I feel like that's *never* a good idea," Penny says.

"We're too exposed moving in a big group and we've got a lot of ground to cover. Franny, take Alpha team and find the electrical box. It's probably in the basement."

"*Oi!* Aren't we looking for a safe?"

Franny winks at me. "We're on it, Sergeant." I watch as they head off and then Bravo team and I keep searching room by room for the safe.

CHAPTER 13
WHERE THERE'S A WILL...

Location: Mr. Mocoso's Mansion
Date: 6JUL20
Time: 0315 hours

I lead Bravo team down a long hallway. There are tall stained-glass windows on both sides. Lights on the wall line the hallway. I can see Hans and Heinz at the end of the hallway, which leads outside to the courtyard. We hug the wall and wait. Alpha team should almost be in the basement.

"What are we waiting for?" Penny whispers to me softly.

"Once the lights go out, we need to double time into the library. That's where Simon thought the safe and will would be hidden."

I've got one eye on Heinz and the other on Hans as they pace near the courtyard, guarding Mr. Mocoso, who is in the library nearby.

Suddenly the light above me flickers and then,

one by one, they turn off and I know Alpha team has found the electrical box. Even in the dark, I can see Hans and Heinz abandon their posts to see what's going on in the basement.

"Let's move out!" I shout to Bravo team.

We race down the hallway and burst into the library where Mr. Mocoso is located.

"Hans, Heinz, is that you?" Mr. Mocoso calls, but he can't see anything with the lights out.

But I can see just fine in the dark. I watch him as he stands up from his big wingback leather chair at his desk. He bumps into some furniture and then grabs a flashlight, shining it around aimlessly. I look around for somewhere to hide, but it's too late.

His flashlight lights us up.

"Look at what the cat dragged in," he says with a menacing grin. He approaches us slowly, backing us into the corner. I step in front of Penny and Brick.

"Who sent you? Was it Ms. Becca?"

I start barking and howling loudly at him to scare him, but it's no use. We're cornered.

"Right back to the pound you go, you filthy, no good, mangy—" he says, grabbing a big burlap sack to throw us in.

All of a sudden, I hear a loud *CRASH* from the chandelier.

I look up and there he is. "Simon!" Penny calls out.

In one motion, Simon swoops down from the chandelier, sending Mr. Mocoso to the ground, knocking him out cold.

"You're a lifesaver," I tell Simon.

"Anything for my old friend Penny," Simon signals. "Did you find the will?" He signals to me again.

"Not yet. I scanned the entire place, but there's nothing in plain sight," I tell him.

"That's because you're looking in *plain* sight," he signals.

I watch as Simon climbs up to the top of the bookshelf. He runs his hands over the books as though he is searching for something. Then he pulls on a book and jumps back off the shelf. We watch as the entire shelf swings open, revealing a hidden room with a safe. We all walk into the room and gather around the safe.

"*Oi!* Does anyone know the code?" Brick asks.

"It's his birthday. He was always making us celebrate it with him," Simon signals, and then begins spinning the dial.

Just like that, the safe pops open and Simon pulls out a rolled-up piece of paper.

"That's it?" Penny asks.

Simon nods and gives Penny the will.

I nudge Penny and say, "I told you there was nothing to it."

"*Oi!* Let's get Alpha team and get out of here!" Brick says.

"Yeah, before this meanie monster wakes up," Penny says, pointing to Mr. Mocoso.

"Come on, Pawtriots, let's move out," I say.

And as we turn around to make our way out of Mr. Mocoso's library, we're met by two big, nasty, drooling pinschers: Hans and Heinz.

"Drop the will, Penny dearest," says Hans.

"Did you really think you could *actually* save the Sanctuary? I'll be sure to have you all back in the pound by morning," says Heinz.

They begin getting closer to us, backing us up into the library.

"I'm not giving it to you," Penny says.

Hans and Heinz smile at each other. "Then things are about to get messy," Heinz says.

I step in between Penny and the pinschers.

"Would you look at this, Heinz? The freak thinks he's a hero," Hans says.

"You've got a wheel now, big deal," Hans scoffs at me.

"No, I've got friends now," I say, pointing behind them. "The Pawtriots."

They spin around and shudder when they see Alpha team looming behind them.

"Things are about to get very messy indeed," Franny says.

Alpha team walks closer to Hans and Heinz and, just like that, the tables have turned: The pinschers are surrounded.

Hans points to Mr. Mocoso, "It was him!"

"Yeah, it was all his fault. He *made* us do it!" Heinz says.

"Please don't hurt us!" Hans says.

"We're not going to hurt you. That's not what being a Pawtriot is about. But seeing as how quickly you flipped on your master, I don't trust you. Franny, tie them up so they can't follow us. And don't worry, once Mr. Mocoso wakes up, he'll free them."

"With pleasure, Sergeant," Franny says, and quickly ties up the two pinschers.

"Pawtriots, *pop smoke*," I say. That's Army-talk for "let's leave . . . and quickly!" We make our way out of the library, locking the door behind us, and head for the fountain.

MISSION ACCOMPLISHED.

Location: Mr. Mocoso's Fountain
Time: 0330 hours

"We did it! We did it! I can't believe we actually did it!" Penny howls out, her smile ear to ear.

Brick plops down on the grass. "So soft, so

perfect," he says, and then promptly falls asleep. Simon uses him as a pillow.

I watch as Morgan and Smithers lie on their backs and look up at the stars. Franny and Sawyer look at each other for a moment and then Franny breaks into a smile and the two friends hug.

I just sit back and soak in my surroundings and let my mind drift a bit. This reminds me of that night in the rain forest with the local villagers after we saved the day there. We sat around that great big fire, celebrating our victory. That was the last time I wore a US Army uniform. That was the last time I saw Kris. That was the night of the big explosion . . .

I swear I can almost smell that fire . . .

Suddenly I am jolted from my daydream. I *can* smell a fire.

"Hey, Franny, what did you use to tie up Hans and Heinz?"

"The rope I got from the electrical box."

"I don't think that was rope," I say, and begin sprinting back into the mansion.

I can hear Penny calling out my name as I rush inside.

I break open the door to the library only to be met by roaring flames and a wall of smoke.

CHAPTER 14
THE SANCTUARY

Location: The Sanctuary, Washington, DC
Date: 14JAN21
Time: 1130 hours

It's been six months since Mr. Mocoso's mansion burned down.

Don't worry. I saved him and Hans and Heinz.

I know what you're thinking: *Why would you save Mr. Mocoso and his two nasty pinschers???*

Because that's what being a Pawtriot is all about: saving others from harm. It's about honor and integrity and doing what's right. And even if they are the bad guys, once the enemy surrenders, they must be treated with dignity and respect.

Penny got the will to Ms. Becca and, just like that, everything went back to normal—minus the visits from Mr. Mocoso! And we were happy to learn that Ms. Becca was able to save the puppies from the pound, too.

Ms. Becca was so impressed by what the Pawtriots were able to do for her that she wrote to the local paper. Then a journalist came by the Sanctuary and wrote an article for the paper. The national news picked up the story and soon the Pawtriots were a household name. A couple of days ago, we even started getting fan mail.

Funny thing is, all these animals are writing to me, asking if they can come to Washington, DC, to join the Pawtriots, but some of them are worried they are too small, or too young, or too weak.

I write them all back and tell them my story, just the way I told it to you. I tell them all about Kris, the villagers, the explosion, even me losing my leg. I tell them about how I ended up here at the Sanctuary, and then at the pound. I tell them about Sergeant First Class Chaps and the Beast he wrestled. And I tell them about the wheel he gave me so we could save the Sanctuary. And lastly, I tell them that it doesn't matter if you're small, young, weak, or even missing a leg—it's what's on the inside that counts. You have to have heart! That's what makes a true Pawtriot.

And I always sign my letters the same way:

Welcome aboard, recruit!
—Sergeant "Rico" Ricochet